All rights reserved. Published by Scholastic Inc., *Publishers since 1920.* SCHOLASTIC and associated logos are trademarks and/or registered trademarks of Scholastic Inc.

The publisher does not have any control over and does not assume any responsibility for author or third-party websites or their content.

This book is a work of fiction. Names, characters, places, and incidents are either the product of the author's imagination or are used fictitiously, and any resemblance to actual persons, living or dead, business establishments, events, or locales is entirely coincidental.

ISBN 978-1-338-79633-9

10 9 8 7 6 5 4 3 2 1   22 23 24 25 26
Printed in China   38
First printing 2022
Book design by Elliane Mellet
Illustrated by Parker-Nia Gordon and Lhaiza Morena

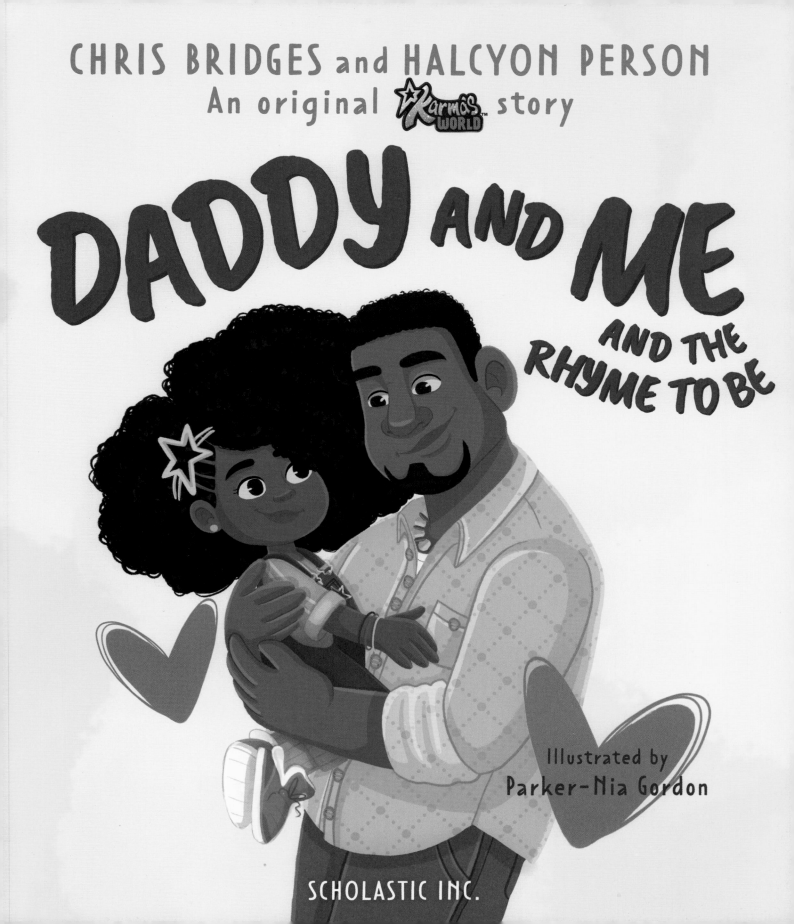

CHRIS BRIDGES and HALCYON PERSON
An original *Karma's World* story

DADDY AND ME
AND THE RHYME TO BE

Illustrated by
Parker-Nia Gordon

SCHOLASTIC INC.

Hi, my name's Karma! I'm seven years old, and I love making music! One day, I'm gonna change the world with my songs!

I might not be there yet, but I know I will someday.

Daddy thinks so. He says, "I believe in you, Kar-Star!"

My daddy is a musician. He teaches everyone in my neighborhood how to play songs! And he makes his own music, too. Hip-hop music is his favorite!

It's the kind of music that makes you wanna get up and dance. The kind of music that flows just right. It kinda sounds like . . .

BOOM CHH CHH CHH

And when we hear that beat, me and Daddy know just what to do . . .

BOOM CHH CHH CHH!

"WHENEVER WE BAKE BROWNIES, I'M THE ONE WHO STIRS THE BATTER."

"AND I'M THE ONE WHO HAS TO CLEAN WHENEVER THE BATTER SPLATTERS."

"WHENEVER WE RIDE BIKES, HE CATCHES ME IF I FALL!"

"YOU'RE MY KAR-STAR, I'M ALWAYS THERE WHEN YOU CALL."

"WHENEVER WE PLAY PRETEND, I'M A DRAGON WHO ROAAARS!"

"YOU KNOW THAT DRAGON BREATH WILL MAKE A PIRATE GO YARRRGH!"

"WHENEVER WE MAKE PICTURES, DADDY'S GOOD AT DRAWING CURLS."

"KARMA, I LOVE YOU—YOU'RE MY WHOLE WIDE WORLD."

Tomorrow is Daddy's birthday, and I want
to surprise him with a special gift.
An awesome gift! The best gift
anyone's given anybody, ever!

So I think and think and think . . .
and then I have a great idea!

I'll write him a song! It'll be the first song I ever write by myself . . . and it'll be all about Daddy.

But when I try to make the music . . .

. . . Nothing sounds right. I even asked my little brother, Keys, for help . . .

But that sounded even worse!

So I try to write the rhymes instead. These rhymes have to be so great, so amazing, so perfect . . .

That they show Daddy just how much I love him.

Lemme try.

I LOVE IT WHEN ME AND DADDY STIR BATTER WITH A SPOON . . .

Uh oh . . . what rhymes with spoon?!

ON THE **MOON!**

No, that's not right!
How about . . .

AND ONCE, WE FLEW AROUND THE WORLD IN A
HOT-AIR BALLOON!

That's not right, either. Lemme try another rhyme!

HE MAKES ME FEEL SAFE FROM
WHEN I SLEEP TO WHEN I WAKE . . .

AND AT NIGHT HE TUCKS ME IN UNDER A GIANT PANCAKE!

UGHHH! That's not it!

DADDY'S ALWAYS THERE, AND HE ALWAYS HAS MY BACK . . .

I JUST LOVE HIM SO MUCH, I WANNA SAY—

QUACK!

No, no, no! I don't wanna say quack!

I've been working and working on my song for Daddy, but nothing I do sounds right. It turns out writing songs is harder than I thought. Especially making up the rhyme!

Maybe I won't ever find the perfect rhyme that tells him just how much I love him. Maybe I'm not good enough.

Maybe I should just give up . . .

"Kar-Star, what's wrong?" Daddy asks, wrapping me in a hug.

I tell him everything. I tell him about his present, and how I wanted it to be a surprise. I tell him that I wish I could write the most amazing song for him that explains exactly how much I love him, but I keep messing up.

"Oh, baby. I already know how much you love me . . . and I love you right back.

"And you know what? Writing a song is hard! It's still hard for me, even after all these years." He pulls me in closer. "But every day, you'll get a little better. And every day, I'll be here to help."

Daddy says maybe we should try something different. "This time I'll say the first line, and you make up the rhyme."

I'm not so sure . . . The rhyme's the hardest part! But Daddy says, "I believe in you, Kar-Star."

BOOM CHH CHH CHH

BOOM

Together, we start to make music. And it makes me wanna dance, and it flows just right! It sounds like . . .

BOOM CHH CHH CHH

CHH CHH CHH

BOOM CHH CHH CHH!

"DADDY AND DAUGHTER, WE ARE THE PERFECT PAIR!"

"I LOVE WHEN DADDY PUTS CLIPS IN MY HAIR!"

"WE LOVE THE SAME GAMES, AND WE LOVE THE SAME SNACKS!"

"BUT ONE THING'S FOR SURE—WE DON'T EVER SAY QUACK!"

"KARMA'S THE RHYME QUEEN, NOTHING'S STOPPING THIS GIRL!"

"DADDY, I LOVE YOU—YOU'RE MY WHOLE WIDE WORLD."

"KARMA MAKES ME FEEL LIKE THE LUCKIEST DAD."
"HAPPY BIRTHDAY, I HOPE THIS IS THE BEST YOU'VE EVER HAD."

"Woohoohoo! You did it Kar-Star! *You* made the rhymes!"
I smile big, and I feel really proud. I guess I can write a song!

"Thank you, Kar-Star. That's the best gift I've ever gotten," Daddy says. "You're gonna write so many amazing songs by yourself one day. But for now, I'm just happy I can be here to help."

I know someday I'm gonna change the world with my music. And I know Daddy's always gonna be there, cheering me on.